Missing Nimâmâ

Melanie Florence

Illustrated by
François Thisdale

CLOCKWISE
PRESS

Published in Canada by Clockwise Press Inc., 201 Taylor Mils Drive North, Richmond Hill, Ontario L4C 2T5

www.clockwisepress.com

solange@clockwisepress.com   christie@clockwisepress.com

10 9 8 7 6 5 4 3 2 1

Library and Archives Canada Cataloguing in Publication
Florence, Melanie, author

Missing nimama / Melanie Florence ; François Thisdale, illustrator.

ISBN 978-0-9939351-4-5 (bound)

I. Thisdale, François, 1964-, illustrator II. Title.

PS8611.L668M57 2015   jC813'.6   C2015-904873-7

Design by CommTech Unlimited
Cover illustration by François Thisdale
Printed in China by Sheck Wah Tong

Job #80826

The text in this book uses OpenDyslexic and Minion Pro typefaces.

For additional resources and an educators' guide to this book, visit www.clockwisepress.com.

As always, for Joshua and Taylor. And finally, for Chris. - M.F.

For Clairette and Monique. - F.T.

As you read through *Missing Nimâmâ*, look closely at the artwork and watch for these words in the Cree language:

ᓂᒫᒫ - nimâmâ (my mother)

ᑲᒫᒫᑯᐢ - kamâmakos (butterfly)

ᓄᐦᑯᒼ - nôhkom (grandmother)

ᐊᓂᓯᐣ - wanisin (she is lost)

ᓂᑖᓂᐢ - nitânis (my daughter)

She dreams. And dreams some more.
In dreams she finds me and she's just a girl again,
her hair in braids, listening to her nôhkom
telling trickster stories around the fire.
Eating bannock and licking the salty grease off her fingers.
Leaning against a mother, her nimâmâ
that she will lose all over again.
When she wakes.

"*Tân'tê nimâmâ?*" I ask nôhkom.
"Where is my mother?"
"Lost", she says. *Lost?*
"If she's lost, let's just go find her."
Nôhkom smooths my hair, soft and dark
as a raven's wing.
Parts it. Braids it. Ties it with a red ribbon.
My mother's favourite colour.
"She's one of the lost women, *kamâmakos.*"
She calls me "little butterfly." Just like nimâmâ did.
Before she got lost.

Taken.
Taken from my home. Taken from my family.
Taken from my daughter.
My kamâmakos. My beautiful little butterfly,
I fought so hard to get back to you, Kateri.
I wish I could tell you that.
And when I couldn't fight anymore, I closed my eyes.
And saw your beautiful face.

My teacher said that my blue dress is pretty.
I drew a picture for nôhkom after we had a snack
and Miss Howard said it was beautiful.
She taught us a song about rainbows at school.
I sang it to nôhkom when she picked me up,
and I gave her the picture I drew.
Going to school is even better than I thought —
I can't wait for tomorrow to come.

She looked so small standing beside her grandmother,
holding her hand so tightly. I wish her other hand
had been in mine as the three of us
walked her into her classroom to meet Miss Howard.
I knew instantly that Kateri would adore her.
I'd worried that she'd cling to her nôhkom,
but she kissed her goodbye
and flitted away
to explore her class.

My class is making cards for Mother's Day.
Drawing hearts with waxy crayons
and pasting bright tissue paper flowers
with white glue that smells funny and drips in thick globs
onto their desks. Maya draws stick figures on her card.
A little girl in a bright yellow dress, just like hers.
A smiling woman stands beside her.
MOMMY, she slowly writes in block letters, her pink tongue
poking out as she works. She sees me watching
and stares down at my blank paper.
"You don't have a mommy," she says.
"Yes, I do!" I tell her, quickly drawing my own stick figures and
trying hard to remember her smile.

My heart aches for her. My beautiful girl. My kamâmakos.
I will always be your mother, Kateri.
Even if I'm not there, sleeping, dreaming of you,
while you make me a special surprise breakfast,
with a card on a tray.
Even if you sometimes forget my face.
Just look in the mirror, my love.
You have your mother's smile.

Nôhkom is teaching me to make fry bread.
I help to measure flour into her mixing bowl.
"Your mother loved to cook with me
when she was your age," she says.
"Does nimâmâ speak Cree?" I ask.
"She does," nôhkom says. "Just like you."
"Did you tell her trickster stories, like you tell me?"
"Of course, kamâmakos. She liked *Wisahkecahk* stories best."
"Just like me!" I say. "Did you teach her beadwork
and shawl dance?"
"I did." Nôhkom smiles at me.
"Your mother is a beautiful dancer, Kateri. Just like you."
"Can we look at your photo albums, nôhkom?" I ask.
She wipes her hands and takes one off the shelf.
I climb off my chair and onto her lap and turn the pages,
looking at my mother. When she was little,
she looked just like me.

Thank you, nimâmâ. Thank you for taking on my child,
though you were finished raising your own years ago.
Thank you for cooking and cleaning and doing laundry
and buying birthday gifts and drying tears.
For loving her unconditionally.
Thank you for telling Kateri about me.
For sharing stories about her mother with her.
For reminding her how much very I love her.
For not letting her forget me.

"Nimâmâ!" My heart beats like a drum. "Mommy!"
 But nôhkom comes instead, because nimâmâ is lost.
"Shhhh, kamâmakos. I'm here."
Nôhkom smooths my hair back
and wipes salty tears off my cheeks.
"It was just a dream."
"Please leave the light on, nôhkom," I beg.
"I don't like the dark."

So dark.
Dark in the room he took me to.
Dark when he left me. And so dark after.
I never saw a light or a tunnel. Only darkness.
Until my daughter's voice called me back.

I smelled your perfume today, nimâmâ. The wind blew
just right and I caught a quick hint of White Musk.
I was in the garden, picking beans for nôhkom and I swear
I heard you laugh.
I turned, half expecting to see you.
Arms open. Telling me that you were home.
But there was no one there. And a moment later,
your perfume was gone too.

But I know you were there
for a second...

I'm here, kamâmakos.
I've never left you.
When you feel me with you, I'm there.
You're never alone.
Your mother is still watching over you.

There was a surprise waiting on my bed
when I got home from school today.
The most beautiful dress
I've ever seen —
All golden and soft and swirly.
I tried it on and stared at myself in the mirror,
then floated down to the kitchen
where nôhkom was making dinner.
I threw my arms around her,
breathing in the familiar scent of lavender soap.

My heart aches when I see them like this.
There's no room for me
in that embrace. I wasn't the one
who found the perfect dress for her first dance.
But I have to smile.
You are so wonderful with her, mother.
Never doubt that you have done
your very best
to raise an amazing woman.
For both of us.

I can't stop smiling.
From the moment I met him,
I haven't been able to wipe the smile off my face.
I feel all of those fairy tale feelings when I'm with him.
"You look like her," he said, pointing at your picture.
"I wish you had known her," I said.
He kissed my hand. "I do know her, Kat.
Because I know you."
You'd love him, Mom.

It's not fair! I lost everything that night.
I had people I loved. People who loved me.
I deserve more than to watch from a distance.
Her new-found love only reminds me
of everything I've lost.
And all that she will still discover.
Oh, be happy, Kateri. Be happy enough for both of us.

Everyone is waiting. Shifting on their foldout chairs.
Fidgeting. Chatting. Smiling.
I take a deep breath and adjust my veil, then smile
as my nôhkom walks into the room.
She holds out a small blue box.
"It was your mother's."
She smiles. Still sad after all these years.
"Your father gave it to her."
I kiss her cheek and hug her close.
"Thank you, nôhkom." *For everything.*
She holds her arm out to me.
"Time to walk you down the aisle, my girl," she says.

She's so beautiful. This breathtaking young woman.
I can't believe this is my little girl, my kamâmakos,
walking down the aisle, wearing my necklace.
My daughter whose life will be so different from mine.
My daughter who has made me proud
every moment of her life.
My daughter who gets to live
happily ever after.

I let out a long breath, trying to imagine
the baby fluttering inside me.
I run my hands over my flat stomach
and picture it large and round.
I close my eyes and imagine our baby —
with my nose
and Daniel's light hair.

I'm going to be a grandmother? A nôhkom!
I still remember you moving inside of me. Kicking me.
I would rub my stomach while you poked me
with a foot or an elbow. I sang to you.
To the thought of you. The dream of you.
Rocking and singing,
aching to hold you.
My little butterfly...
you're going to be
a wonderful mother.

I wasn't expecting to see so many people here.
Holding signs. Wearing t-shirts. Sharing stories.
I'm surrounded by the faces of so many
Aboriginal women who never came home.
Stolen sisters.
I hold my own sign. My own lost loved one.
Nimâmâ. *Aiyana Cardinal.*
Missing. Lost.

So many faces. So many lost souls. So many people left behind. Wondering if their loved one will ever come home. Or having to live with the knowledge that they never will. Too many lost and not enough who care.

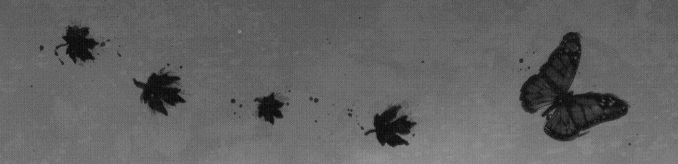

Once upon a time, there was a girl,
a little butterfly
who flew to the phone every time it rang.
Hoping against hope
that her mother was coming home.
The phone rang today. I didn't run.
I had stopped running long ago,
hoping against hope.
"We found your mother," they said.
My heart nearly pounded out of my chest
for a moment,
hoping against hope.
But I knew she was gone. I had known for years.
Still, I cried.

I'm so sorry, Kateri.
I wish there could have been
a happier ending for you.
I wish I could have come home.
But I'm here. I've watched you grow up
into a beautiful, kind, wonderful woman.
I'm at peace with that now.

It's not the ending we dreamed of.

But it will be happy enough, kamâmakos.

Many Voices

Although Kateri and Aiyana Cardinal's story is a work of fiction, there are far too many families like theirs, waiting for a mother, sister, daughter, or aunt who will never come home. In the true story of the hundreds of missing and murdered indigenous women of Canada, there are many groups of voices.

There are the voices of the women themselves and the families and friends who love them.

"I have a picture of her in my room and I do remember her and think of her almost daily. It's an experience you wouldn't really wish on anyone. It's just…it's heartbreaking."

> -Alex Cywink, brother of Sonya Cywink

There is the voice of the international community, which has been watching Canada's response to the crisis.

"The measures taken to prevent and protect Aboriginal women from disappearances and murders have been insufficient and inadequate…
"Gender-based violence seriously inhibits Aboriginal women's capacity and that of their children to enjoy their rights and freedoms…"
Canada must "take measures to establish a National Public Inquiry into cases of missing and murdered Aboriginal women and girls."

> -United Nations Committee on the Elimination of Discrimination
> Against Women Report, March 2015

The violence inflicted on Aboriginal women is often rooted in the deep socio-economic inequalities and discrimination their communities face, which can be traced back to the period of colonization.

There are the voices of government and law enforcement authorities tasked with protecting all citizens and seeing that justice is done.

"It isn't really high on our radar, to be honest."
"We brought in laws across this country that I think are having more effect, in terms of crimes of violence against not just aboriginal women, but women and persons more generally. And we remain committed to that course of action."

> - Prime Minister Stephen Harper on his refusal to call for a national inquiry.

"Now is the time to take action, not to continue to study the issue."

> -Justice Minister Peter MacKay, reconfirming that the federal government
> does not intend to set up a public inquiry.

Highway 16 in northern British Columbia, where so many indigenous women and girls have been murdered or disappeared, has come to be known as the Highway of Tears.

"It is time for the prime minister and [Aboriginal Affairs Minister] Bernard Valcourt to stop ignoring the sociological phenomenon of missing and murdered indigenous women and take federal action to address the crisis."

> - NDP Aboriginal Affairs critic Jean Crowder

And there are the voices of the Canadian people…

"We're not seeing any change, any improvement in the situation. We are calling for a national public inquiry and we will continue to call for that. This just can't go on."

> -Claudette Dumont-Smith, executive director of the Native Women's Association of Canada

If you would like to find out more information about the Stolen Sisters and add your voice to the growing number around the world, calling for action, visit the No More Stolen Sisters site at Amnesty International.
http://www.amnesty.ca/our-work/issues/indigenous-peoples/no-more-stolen-sisters

The Numbers

- A total of 1181 Indigenous women and girls have been murdered or went missing between 1980 and 2012.
- 1017 are homicide victims, representing about 16% of all female homicides across Canada.
- Indigenous women and girls make up 4.3 percent of the total female population but make up 11.3 percent of the murdered and missing.
- As of April 2015, 174 Aboriginal women across all police jurisdictions remain missing, 111 of these under suspicious circumstances.
- Of cases solved: 85% of Aboriginal cases compared to 89% of non-Aboriginal cases.

Source: RCMP Updated Report on Missing and Murdered Aboriginal Women (2015)